I0757486

POTATO
SCHOOL

Long ago, in the mountains of Idaho, the first
potatoes were planted, setting the stage
for the beginning of the Famous Idaho Potato.
Packin' Spuds is an illustrated story of the
history of the Idaho Potato, told through a
lesson by Mrs. Russet, as she educates the
potato kids in her class at the Potato School.
Packin' Spuds represents the mythical and
elusive "Super Potato," that is resistant to
the diseases that still are a concern for potato
farmers everywhere. This fun-filled potato
character is "packin'" (a set of
pistols) to fight back against the
devastation of
diseases takin'
potatoes down!

Packin' Spuds
The History of the
IDAHO
POTATO
by
Dr.
Graham

Staghorn Ridge Publications

Packin' Spuds: The History of the IDAHO POTATO
by Dr. Graham

Author Contact Information:
E-mail: staghornridge@gmail.com
www.facebook.com/DrGrahamStories
Harrison, ID

ISBN-13: 978-0986158803
Library of Congress Control Number: 2015902432

Written and Illustrated by Dr. Carol J. Graham

Staghorn Ridge Publications, Harrison, ID

Packin' Spuds

"A long time ago, near the mouth of the pristine Clearwater River, our ancestors were first planted in the state of Idaho," Mrs. Russet began reading.

"But where did Packin' Spuds grow up?" asked Norkotah, known for her distinctive earthy potato flavor.

"We will learn more about Packin' Spuds, our famous 'Super Potato' hero as we read more together," Mrs. Russet explained. An enormous poster of Packin' Spuds was proudly displayed on the classroom wall.

Packin' Spuds

⌘　⌘　⌘

"In the year 1837, Henry Spaulding, a missionary, taught the Nez Perce Indians how to plant potatoes. But the area was very mountainous, and did not have good soil, so we did not grow very well. Can anyone tell me how we grow best?"

"I know! I know!" Yellow Finn said excitedly. "We need high moisture in the soil, warm days and cool nights!" he answered matter-of-factly.

"Yes, and there is one more very important part," Mrs. Russet said.

"I remember!" Yukon Gold blurted out, as he stood up proudly. He was well known for his yellow, buttery and moist potato flavor. "We need lots of rich minerals from the volcanic ash."

⌘ ⌘ ⌘

"Yes, that's right. Now getting back to our story…," continued Mrs. Russet, "the second time we were known to have been planted in Idaho turned out to be an accident."

"Oh no…!" exclaimed the children potatoes with a fearful look on their faces. "What happened?"

Teacher

"Well…," went on Mrs. Russet, "during the summer of 1860, some early colonists settled in Franklin County, Idaho, but they thought they were still in Utah. This is considered to be the first permanent planting of us, and possibly the first planting of our 'Super Potato' hero, Packin' Spuds."

"Packin' Spuds was born in Franklin County, Idaho, Mrs. Russet?" asked Yukon Gold, who always had a lot of questions.

⌘ ⌘ ⌘

"No one knows for sure. However, we do know that no one has been able to grow us as well as the first-year crop grown on desert soil. They have not been able to figure out exactly what the desert soil contains after centuries of being a desert. We do know that the very first planting produces an exceptional crop. It is possible that Packin' Spuds came from that first-year crop, making him special, indeed."

"Why is Packin' Spuds packin'?" asked Yellow Finn.

"That's an interesting question, Yellow Finn," Mrs. Russet said.

But before she could answer, Yukon Gold piped up, "He's packing guns 'cause he wants to protect us from all of the bad things that happen to us potatoes!"

Teacher

"Well…in a way, Yukon Gold is right," Mrs. Russet replied. "Packin' Spuds is very upset about the diseases that cause us not to grow or survive as we should. He wants us to be healthy and fights for us to be disease free and treated with respect." Then, Mrs. Russet pointed to Packin' Spuds, proudly displayed on the classroom wall.

Packin' Spuds

⌘ ⌘ ⌘

Turning the page, Mrs. Russet began reading again. "Most of us that grow in Idaho today are of one kind, which is called the Russet Burbank. This kind of potato is known throughout the world as the famous traditional Idaho Baker. I am a very proud descendent of the Russet Burbank seedling that Luther Burbank found in 1872."

"Why is Packin' Spuds called the 'famous Super Potato?'" asked Norkotah, dressed to show off her famously attractive medium-brown color and oblong shape.

Russet
Burbank

⌘ ⌘ ⌘

Mrs. Russet smiled, then said, "Well…no one knows for sure, but people think it is because he has survived all the diseases and rough handling that can make us ugly, bruised, and disfigured. And in some cases…," Mrs. Russet whispered, softly lowering her voice, "these problems cause us not to survive to grow at all.

"Packin' Spuds is believed to have survived for more than 150 years," Mrs. Russet beamed, "<u>even</u> through the terrible Potato Scab Outbreak in the early 1900's!"

Bruised Potato

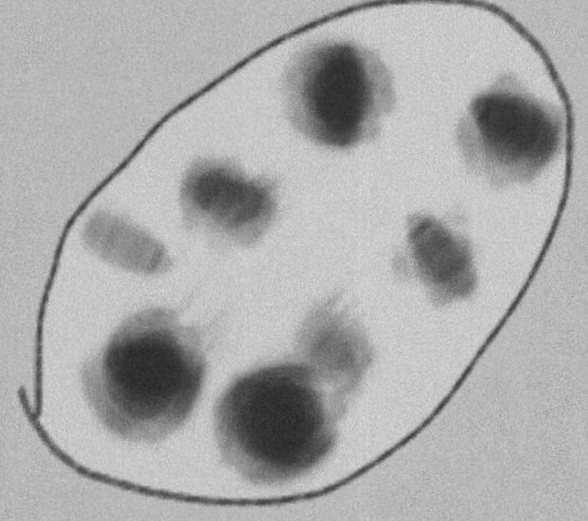

Disfigured Potato

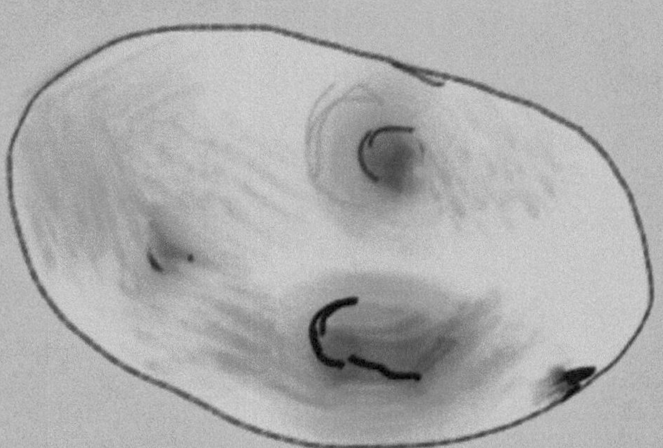

Potato Scab

Healthy Potato

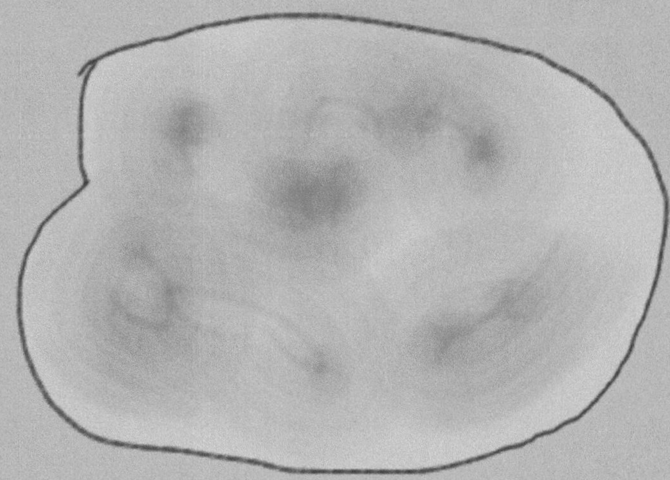

"What happened to us then?" whispered Yukon Gold, peeking through one scared eye.

Mrs. Russet began reading again, "The problem with Scab is that it leaves crust-like spots on the potato and people do not want us. That is why we attend Potato School in Pocatello…to learn all that we can so that we grow to be beautiful, strong and delicious. Everyone is looking for the 'Super Potato,' which is a potato that grows even better than me, the Russet Burbank. Packin' Spuds might be the 'Super Potato' everyone has been looking for all this time."

Potato School
EDUCATION FOR:
Health, Flavor
and Beauty

"Is Packin' Spuds related to Joe Marshall?" Norkotah asked, as she smoothed out an eye that was sticking up a bit too far. Looking up shyly, she continued, "My mother told me that Joe Marshall is known as the 'Idaho Potato King' because he made sure we were of the highest quality, and that Packin' Spuds is a distant relative."

"Yes, Norkotah," Mrs. Russet said. "Mr. Marshall had an understanding of the importance of us coming from certified seed potatoes. This means that the best seed potatoes are to be used for planting."

Key Point -
"Potato King"
Joe Marshall
Certified Seed Potatoes

"Mr. Marshall is no longer with us, but we can thank him for everything he has done to make us healthy, beautiful and delicious. Today, we are known around the world for being the best potatoes."

"But, is Packin' Spuds Mr. Marshall's cousin?" asked Yukon Gold, waving his hand with excitement.

"Hmm…" Mrs. Russet stopped and put one finger to her lips. "Yukon Gold, you might have an idea there."

POTATO SCHOOL

⌘ ⌘ ⌘

Author and Illustrator
Dr. Carol J. Graham

Dr. Carol J. Graham is a National Board Certified Reading and Language Arts Teacher Specialist. She is an elementary teacher, and principal, who lives in Coeur d' Alene, Idaho. As principal and a teacher at Hometown Elementary School (West Virginia), her leadership and experience spirited Hometown Elementary School to be recognized at the state and national levels.

As a teacher, her students achieved acclaim as finalists in a National NASA competition and several national STEM awards. As principal, Hometown Elementary was selected as a National Green Ribbon School, National Title I School, West Virginia School of Excellence, and West Virginia Distinguished School during her tenure.

Beautiful Echo Ranch, near Kalispell, Montana, provided many childhood and young adult experiences for Dr. Graham. She fondly remembers riding her registered quarter horse, "Whimper Duke," many miles throughout the open range herding cattle. Later, she attended Montana State University to attain her degree in teaching.

As a teacher in Idaho, her interactions with the children and teachers of the state, as well as her wealth of experiences from the state of West Virginia, provide the setting and backdrop for many of Dr. Graham's stories.